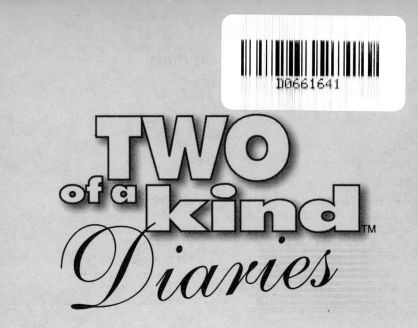

TWO of a kind™
Diaries

Win a
sterling silver
charm bracelet!
Details on page 95.

Look for more

titles:

TWO of a kind™
Diaries
Wish on a Star

by Louise A. Gikow
from the series created by
Robert Griffard & Howard Adler

HarperEntertainment
An Imprint of HarperCollinsPublishers
A PARACHUTE PRESS BOOK

A PARACHUTE PRESS BOOK

Parachute Publishing, L.L.C.
156 Fifth Avenue
Suite 302
New York, NY 10010

Published by
HarperEntertainment
An Imprint of HarperCollins*Publishers*
10 East 53rd Street, New York, NY 10022-5299

TWO OF A KIND books created and produced by
Parachute Press, L.L.C., in cooperation with Dualstar Publications,
a division of Dualstar Entertainment Group, LLC,
published by HarperEntertainment, an imprint of HarperCollins Publishers.

ISBN 0-06-059592-2

HarperCollins®, ® , and HarperEntertainment™ are trademarks of HarperCollins Publishers Inc.

First printing: April 2005

Printed in the United States of America

Visit HarperEntertainment on the World Wide Web at
www.harpercollins.com

10 9 8 7 6 5 4 3 2 1

Chapter 1

Wednesday

Dear Diary,

I am totally mixed up!

Today, I got the coolest assignment from Ms. Lewis. But then something happened that made me think it wasn't going to be cool at all.

Hold it. I'm telling this all backward. Let me start from the beginning. . . .

You know Ms. Lewis, Diary. She teaches Social Sciences to us First Formers—seventh graders— here at the White Oak Academy for Girls. That's the boarding school I go to with my sister, Ashley.

Anyway, this semester, Ms. Lewis announced that we will be doing a unit on animal behavior. (My roommate, Campbell Smith, wanted to know if that meant we would be studying the boys at Harrington Academy. Ha!)

"What it means," Ms. Lewis said, looking at Campbell, "is that each of you will be studying an animal—or a group of animals—and then writing a paper about what you learn. You will write about the animal's diet, habits, likes and dislikes, relation-ships with other animals and people . . . whatever

1

you see. You can take pictures, if you want, or include drawings or anything else you think will make the paper exciting."

Pretty interesting, huh?

But that wasn't the coolest part.

Then Ms. Lewis announced that we weren't just going to go to the library and read about our animals. We were going to actually help take care of the animals for the rest of the month!

But that wasn't the best part either.

Each of us was assigned to a different animal-care place, such as a veterinarian's office or an animal shelter. And *this* is the best part of all, Diary: I've been assigned to Starbright Stables, to take care of my very own—you guessed it—horse!!

You remember Starbright Stables, don't you, Diary? It's the stable just down the road from White Oak, where I rode Sugar, that totally sweet and beautiful mare. Just think: I could look at those bright, intelligent eyes again, brush her soft mane, and take her for a quick trot around the paddock. I've got my fingers crossed that I'll be taking care of Sugar.

Not that it really matters. Whichever horse I get, it's going to be so much fun!

Each of us will be working with a partner. I've been assigned to work with Courtney Spaulding. I don't know her very well. She's new here. But she seems pretty nice. So I guess it'll be okay.

As I grabbed my books after class, my friend Summer Sorenson came over to me. She didn't look very happy. She pushed a strand of her long blond hair behind one ear and frowned. "Where are you working?" she asked me.

After I told her, Summer sighed. "I wish I had gotten that assignment," she said.

"But you don't like horses!" I said, laughing.

"Well, I don't," Summer admitted. "They smell kind of icky. But I," she went on, looking grim, "have to work at a veterinarian's office! And they give shots to animals. You know how scared I am of shots!"

"You're scared of getting them, not giving them." Campbell called out behind us.

Summer turned. "It doesn't matter whether I get them *or* give them!" She moaned. "It gives me the creeps just to think about it! Besides, I think I'm allergic to cats. Every time I go over to my cousin's house, I get hives."

"That's because you don't like your cousin," Campbell said, grinning. She ran her fingers through her short, spiky brown hair. Campbell told us she was assigned to work at an animal shelter.

"Who are you paired up with, Summer?" asked

Phoebe Cahill, Ashley's roommate. She pushed her glasses up on her nose.

"Madison Willis," Summer said.

Phoebe nodded. "She's great," she said. "And isn't her dad a doctor? She's probably used to all that medical stuff like shots and things. She won't mind if you duck out of the room when things get too gross. . . ."

Summer didn't look convinced.

Campbell turned to me. "Who are you working with, Mary-Kate?" she asked.

"Courtney Spaulding," I told her.

"Oh." Phoebe nodded. "The new girl."

Courtney had been at White Oak for the last two weeks. She came here from somewhere in the South—Kentucky, I think. She has greenish-brownish eyes and long dark hair that she always wears in a ponytail.

I looked around for Courtney. I wanted to talk about the assignment and tell her I was happy to be working with her. I finally spotted her over by Ms. Lewis's desk, deep in conversation with Ms. Lewis.

"Excuse me, guys," I said to my friends. "I'll meet you outside. I just want to talk to Courtney for a second. . . ."

Phoebe, Campbell, and Summer headed for the

door. I wandered over to the front of the room to wait until Courtney and Ms. Lewis were finished talking.

As I did, I couldn't help overhearing what Courtney was saying.

"Do I have to?" Courtney was asking. "I can't work at the stables. Please . . . could you give me something else to do? I'll do anything!"

Ms. Lewis looked up at that moment and caught my eye. My face flamed.

"Courtney, we can talk about this in my office," Ms. Lewis said. She picked up her books.

Courtney turned and saw me. "Mary-Kate!" she said, startled. Then she blushed.

"Hey, Courtney!" I said, trying to make her feel better. "I just want you to know that I'm really happy to be working with you."

Courtney smiled, but it didn't look like her heart was in it. "Thanks, Mary-Kate," she said. "But—"

"Courtney?" Ms. Lewis interrupted.

Courtney gave me a worried look. Then she turned and followed Ms. Lewis out of the room.

I stood there, wondering what was going on. Courtney was clearly very upset.

Why didn't she want to work at Starbright Stables?

Dear Diary,

Guess what? Today was the day the headmistress, Mrs. Pritchard, chose the two girls who'll be working in her office this term!

I've told you about it before, Diary—remember? Every term, Mrs. Pritchard "hires" two of the White Oak First Formers to help out in her office for three afternoons a week. She says it's a great way to get us girls really involved in the school.

Everyone wants the job. It's like a big competition. No one really knows how she chooses her helpers, so everyone tries to get the best recommendation from a teacher, or the best grades, or they try to write the best essay saying why they think the job will give them an opportunity to grow and mature.

The real reason everyone wants the job?

The auction.

Okay, pizza night is great, too. It's a White Oak tradition. Every Tuesday night Mrs. Pritchard treats every dorm to pizza instead of regular dinner. The girls who submit the pizza order—Mrs. Pritchard's helpers—get to choose the toppings!

Plus, the office helpers get to know everything that's going on at school before anyone else does.

Sometimes they get to read the announcements during the morning assembly, too.

But as I mentioned, the *real* reason lots of girls apply for the job is the auction. Every year White Oak has an Alumni Auction, which is a big fundraiser event. Lots of people come, wearing glamorous evening gowns and tuxedos. There's a live band and tons of food. And sometimes a famous celebrity makes a surprise visit!

And the only students invited are—you guessed it—the girls who work in Mrs. Pritchard's office.

I submitted my application a month ago, with recommendations from two of my teachers. Plus, I wrote a great essay for my application. My sister, Mary-Kate, said I was sure to get the job.

When it was time for assembly this morning, I raced into the auditorium with my roommate, Phoebe Cahill, and Mary-Kate and her roommate, Campbell Smith. I couldn't wait to hear who'd gotten the job.

Dana Woletsky was standing in the middle of the aisle, talking to Kristen Lindquist and Fiona Ferris. They were making it impossible for anyone to pass.

"I'm sure she'll pick me this time," Dana was saying. "After all, my mother and my grandmother both worked in the office when they went here. Plus, they always contribute something big to the auction."

"Excuse me, Dana," Mary-Kate said loudly.

Dana turned to stare at us. "Mary-Kate." She looked over at me. "Ashley," she said coolly. Then she slowly stepped aside so we could pass.

"Do I detect a slight chill in the air?" Campbell asked as we slipped into seats in the third row.

I frowned. Dana is in what Mary-Kate calls "the snotty crowd." That basically means, Diary, that she thinks she and her friends are better than anyone else here. And rumor had it that she and I were Mrs. Pritchard's top choices for the job.

Dana, Kristen, and Fiona sat down right behind us. "I'm not worried," Dana was saying loudly. "I'm sure to be one of the girls to get chosen."

Then, Mrs. Pritchard stood up onstage and walked to the podium. "Settle down, girls," the headmistress said, raising her hand. Everyone who was still standing quickly scrambled for a seat.

"Now, I know you're all curious as to who will be working in the office this term," Mrs. Pritchard began. "So I'm not going to leave you in suspense any longer."

I leaned forward in my seat. I really wanted the job.

"The first girl chosen is . . . Ashley Burke."

My sister whooped and gave me a quick hug. Campbell gave me a thumbs-up.

"Congratulations, Ashley!" Phoebe whispered. "You're going to have a great time!"

A bunch of other girls turned around and smiled at me, too. I felt great!

Mrs. Pritchard stood there onstage until things settled down again. I wondered if I was going to have to work with Dana.

Dana must have been thinking the same thing. "Nice to have you working with me, Ashley," she said in a stage whisper.

"My second helper this term is"—Mrs. Pritchard looked down at a piece of paper in her hand— "Becky David."

The room fell silent. It wasn't Dana, after all. Heads swiveled, trying to locate Becky.

I turned around, too. Dana's face was bright red. Kristen was saying something to her, and Dana was shaking her head furiously.

Mary-Kate leaned over to me. "Dana really thought she had it," she said quietly. She pushed a strand of strawberry-blond hair behind her ear.

I nodded. Even though I didn't like Dana very much, I felt sorry for her. She must feel really terrible.

But I was really thinking about Becky.

I had to admit, Diary, I was surprised Mrs. Pritchard had chosen her. I don't know Becky very well, but she's supershy. She's known on campus as a bit of a klutz, and a little forgetful, too. She's always late for class or whatever else she's supposed to be doing.

Mrs. Pritchard's voice interrupted my thoughts. "All right, girls, settle down," she said. "I still have a few more announcements to make."

I looked around, trying to find Becky in the crowd, while Mrs. Pritchard read off the morning announcements.

"And that's it for this morning, girls," Mrs. Pritchard finished. "Becky and Ashley, report to my office at three-thirty. Everybody, have a great day!"

As we filed out of the auditorium and headed to our classes, I passed Becky. She was sitting in the back row, twirling her medium-length brown hair with one finger. Her gray eyes looked a little stunned.

"I'll see you later," I told my sister. Then I walked over to Becky. "Hey, congratulations!" I told her. "It'll be fun working with you!"

"Thanks," Becky said with a little smile.

"Yes. Congratulations, Becky." Becky and I both turned to see Dana standing there.

"I hope you do *really* well at the job," Dana said

sweetly, looking at Becky. "Of course, if you run into any trouble . . . well, I'll be glad to help. My mom and grandmother both worked in the head-mistress's office when they went to White Oak, so I know the ropes." Dana's green eyes narrowed. "And I'll be happy to *take over for you* if anything goes wrong."

Becky suddenly stood up. As she did, her books and papers, which she had balanced on her lap, fell to the floor with a thump.

Becky froze for a second. Dana just stared at her, eyebrows raised. Then she gave me a funny look and walked out of the auditorium, shaking her head. On her way out, she said something to Kristen. Kristen looked back at us and laughed.

I bent down and helped Becky pick up her stuff from under the auditorium seats. By the time we were done, everybody had left and the room was empty.

"I'm going to be late for biology!" Becky said in a panicked voice.

"Don't worry," I told her. "You've got plenty of time."

But she raced away without another word.

As I headed down the hall, I thought about what Dana had said.

It had sounded nice enough on the surface. But the way she'd said it—especially the part about taking over if Becky had any problems—well, it had sounded like some kind of threat. I was sure Becky had picked up on it, too.

I knew Dana had counted on getting the job. But there wasn't anything she could do about it now.

Or was there?

Chapter 2

Friday

Dear Diary,

Well, Diary, things have not turned out exactly as I'd planned.

I was so excited when I first found out I'd be working at Starbright Stables! I wanted to start my job as soon as I could. Plus, we only had three weeks before we had to submit an outline of our paper, and only three weeks more after that to write it.

I decided to head over right after school on Thursday.

I went to Courtney's room after my last class let out. After all, we were in this together, and I figured she might want to walk to the stables with me. That is, if she hadn't gotten out of the assignment altogether.

But she wasn't there.

In fact, her roommate, Cyndy Becker, hadn't seen Courtney all afternoon.

"When she gets in, please tell her I'm heading over to the stables," I told Cyndy. "She can meet me there later, if she wants."

When I got to Starbright Stables, I stood outside

the main gate for a minute, looking around. It was as beautiful as I had remembered. The paddock was off toward the left, surrounded by a cheerful white fence. There were bright green grassy fields just beyond, and beyond that were trees and forest paths.

The old gray and white house was straight ahead, and the stables were over on the right behind the house.

Sean O'Reilly, the sixteen-year-old son of the owners, was just coming out of the barn. He was carrying a bucket. The stables' three golden retrievers, Goldy, Cosmo, and Spice, came running out after him. They were always hanging around Sean. He was really great with all sorts of animals, not just horses.

Sean waved at me. "Hey, Mary-Kate!" he called, grinning.

I walked over to meet him. "Hi, Sean!" I said, smiling and leaning down to rub Goldy between the ears. "Nice to see you."

"So you're one of the girls from White Oak who were assigned to help us out, huh?" Sean put down the bucket and wiped his hands on his jeans. "Congratulations!" he said. "Mom and Dad are going to be really glad to have you around. And so will I. Things have been pretty busy around here. . . ."

Just then, Mrs. O'Reilly came out of the house. She had curly red hair and a big, open smile. She walked down the stone path to the gate and gave me a hug. "Mary-Kate! I'm so thrilled you're here," she said happily. "I heard all about your assignment from your teacher. Jack will be delighted, too."

Jack is Mrs. O'Reilly's husband, and the co-owner of Starbright Stables.

"So where's your friend?" Sean asked. "I thought there were two girls who were coming over to help."

"There are," I told him. "I went looking for her before I came over today, but she wasn't around. I left her a message, so maybe she'll show up in a little bit. . . ."

But I wasn't so sure.

"Would you like to meet the horse you're going to take care of?" Sean asked.

"You bet!" I said. "I've had my fingers crossed for the last two days! Is it Sugar?"

Mrs. O'Reilly shook her head. "I'm sorry, dear," she said. "Sugar's being boarded down south this season. You're going to be working with one of our new horses. His name is Rigel."

"Rigel," I said. "That's a funny name."

"Rigel is the name of a star," Mrs. O'Reilly told me. "The star Rigel is in the constellation Orion, the hunter. If you look up at the stars, Rigel is in the place where the hunter Orion's left foot would be. When Rigel the horse was born, his owners thought he'd be quick-footed and confident—a real star. Plus, he has a star on his forehead."

"He sounds terrific," I said.

"He was," Mrs. O'Reilly said, frowning. "But during a jumping competition last season, he fell. There were two yappy little dogs in the stands, and they started to bark just as he took a big fence. He knocked it down and took a bad spill."

I frowned. "Oh, no!" I said. "Was he hurt? And what happened to his rider?"

Mrs. O'Reilly shook her head. "His rider was fine, Mary-Kate. And Rigel wasn't really hurt. But he got badly spooked. He won't jump anything anymore. His owners sent him to us in the hope that we could get him back to himself again—"

"Mary-Kate Burke!" I turned to see Mr. O'Reilly striding toward us from the barn.

He came over and grabbed my hand and pumped it heartily. "I'm glad to see you. So I hear you're going to help us out with Rigel. He's quite a character, you know. He takes about ten times more work than any of the other horses in the stable. Even getting him out of his stall can be a big production."

Mrs. O'Reilly held up her hand. "Let Mary-Kate meet the horse, Jack, before you scare her half to death," she said. She turned to me. "He's a good horse," she said. "It's just that we have our hands full with the other horses . . . and Rigel is a special case."

"Where is he?" I asked.

"In the barn," Sean said. "I'll take you."

I said good-bye to the O'Reillys. "If Courtney shows up," I said, "could you tell her where I am?"

"Of course, dear." Mrs. O'Reilly nodded. She looked down at the dogs. "Suppertime!" she said, clapping her hands, and the three retrievers trotted after her into the house.

As Sean and I walked toward the stables, he shook his head. "I don't know . . ." he began, running his hand through his reddish-brown hair. Then he trailed off.

"Don't know what?" I asked him.

"You'll see," he said simply.

He opened the big wooden doors to the stable, and we went inside. I took a deep breath. It smelled of horses and clean hay and leather. I loved every bit of it.

"Rigel's over in the back stall," Sean said. He began walking down past the other horses. Noses poked out to see who it was, and horses whickered gently as we passed. I patted a few noses of some old friends before I got to the last stall and looked inside.

Rigel was drinking some water. When he heard us, he lifted his head to look at us and pricked his ears forward.

He was a beautiful bay with a white star on his forehead and four white stockings. He slowly walked toward me and stuck his head out over the stable door. Sean backed up a step.

"He's gorgeous!" I said. I reached out and pet the horse gently on his soft muzzle. "You are a star, boy, aren't you?"

"Yup, he is," Sean said, moving closer. "But he can be a real pain." He shook his head. "Like Dad said . . . it takes a ton of time just to make sure he's been fed and exercised every day. Not that he would ever hurt anybody," he added quickly. "He's a sweetie. It's just . . ." His voice trailed off. "Well, you'll see for yourself."

"I'm happy to help out," I told Sean. "I'm sure

Rigel and I will get along just fine. And remember: I won't be alone. There are two of us. Courtney should be here pretty soon."

Sean nodded. "Well, at least Rigel should give you something to write about for that paper of yours. Here. You can feed him these oats." Sean already had a pail half full of oats standing by the stable door. "I have to go muck out a few stalls."

I nodded. "Piece of cake!" I told him.

As Sean moved away, I turned back to Rigel. "You're not going to give me any trouble, are you, boy?" I murmured, rubbing his muzzle again.

Rigel snorted as I picked up the bucket of oats and slowly opened the stall door. I slipped inside and shut it behind me. Rigel nuzzled my hair.

This is *going to be a piece of cake*, I thought, smiling up at the horse. He's just an old softy—

Rigel reached down, plucked my White Oak baseball cap right off my head, and started to chew on it.

"Rigel!" I said, laughing as I put the pail down. I grabbed for my cap and pulled. But Rigel was not about to let go.

We must have looked pretty silly, Diary, playing tug-of-war with my cap. Pretty soon, I realized that I wasn't going to get anywhere. You can't fight over a cap with a two-ton horse . . . and win, that is.

I stopped pulling, and Rigel went back to chewing.

Maybe he's hungry, I thought.

I dumped the bucket of oats into his trough. Then I scooped up a handful and held it out to him with my palm flat, just as I had been taught when I was a little girl. "Here, boy," I said. "Are you hungry?"

Rigel stared at me, still chewing on my cap. Then he turned his body sideways, herded me into a corner of his stall, and *leaned* on me! It didn't hurt—he wasn't really placing any weight on me. But he was clearly telling me who was boss.

"Rigel!" I giggled. "Get *off* me!"

Rigel turned his head to look at me, still chewing on my cap. I slipped under his neck and grabbed his halter, turning around so he was facing me again. Then I opened the stall door and backed out.

Rigel stuck his head over the door and stared out at me. Then he opened his mouth and dropped my cap on the barn floor.

I picked it up. It looked pretty gross.

I was beginning to understand what Sean meant about Rigel. He had a . . . well, let's call it a mischievous streak. And he was stubborn, too.

This wasn't going to be easy. No wonder the O'Reillys wanted me and Courtney to help with him.

And speaking of Courtney—where was she?

Dear Diary,

Poor Becky!

We've just begun our job in Mrs. Pritchard's office and already she's got one strike against her.

Here's what happened.

On Wednesday afternoon, Becky and I headed over to Mrs. Pritchard's office to begin work. We were going to be working Tuesday, Wednesday, and Friday afternoons.

When we got there, Joan, Mrs. Pritchard's secretary, showed us around. Then we waited for Mrs. Pritchard and talked about pizza night.

"Tons of mushrooms, extra cheese, and absolutely *no* anchovies," I told Becky. "That's my favorite." It would be our job to call in the pizza order for the whole school every Tuesday night. We could choose whatever kind of pizza we wanted from Mario's. (They make the best crust ever!)

"That sounds good," Becky said, looking doubtful. When she gets that doubtful look, she reminds me of a little brown mouse. "But I think you should do the ordering, Ashley." She looked at me. I could almost see her little whiskers quiver. "I wouldn't want to mess up or anything."

"Good afternoon, girls!" Mrs. Pritchard's voice interrupted us. Becky jumped.

"Good afternoon, Mrs. Pritchard!" I said. Becky bowed her head. Seriously, Diary, she practically curtsied!

Makeover, I thought. *As soon as we've got some time, I've got to give this girl a makeover.* There was nothing like an Ashley Burke makeover to give a girl some self-confidence!

"So has Joan shown you girls around?" Mrs. Pritchard asked us.

"She just finished," I told her.

"Good. Come into my office." Mrs. Pritchard walked into her office and started to sit down behind her desk.

There was a loud "meow," and Tasha—the big old tabby cat who lives in the office—shot up from the chair and onto the desk.

Mrs. Pritchard shook her head, picked up the cat, and dumped her on the floor. "One of your jobs," she told us as Tasha rubbed up against my shoes, "will be to feed Tasha. The cat food is in the closet.

Give her one cup every day. And make sure her water is changed regularly."

Becky took a little pocket diary out of her backpack and started to write.

Mrs. Pritchard motioned for us to sit. Then she looked at the calendar on her desk. "Okay," she said. "Next Tuesday, Becky, would you please order the pizza?"

Becky gulped. "Are you sure you don't want Ashley to do it?" she asked.

Mrs. P looked up at Becky, surprised. Then she smiled kindly. "I'm sure you'll do a fine job," she said.

Becky nodded and wrote something in her diary.

Mrs. Pritchard sat back in her chair. "Good. Okay. As you know, next to ordering the pizza"—Mrs. P's eyes twinkled—"the biggest part of your job this month is to help me with the White Oak Alumni Auction and Fund-raiser."

I sat up straight. This was the best part.

Mrs. P reached over and pulled a card out of a drawer. She handed it to me. "The girls who work here in the office always help make the auction a huge success. There's a lot to do this term—probably more than at any other time during the school year. But the auction is definitely top priority."

I looked at the card. It was a beautifully designed invitation to this year's auction. It was going to be held in the school auditorium. I handed the card to Becky, who glanced at it and then returned it to Mrs. Pritchard.

"Every year," Mrs. Pritchard went on, "White Oak's very generous alumnae donate all sorts of items that are auctioned off to make money for the school. They can give us tickets to events, meals at restaurants, vacations, books, clothing—all sorts of things. And this year should be our biggest auction ever." Mrs. Pritchard stopped. She looked at us seriously.

"It's also our most important auction in a long time," she went on. "I'm trying to raise the rest of the money to build a new, state-of-the-art science lab."

Becky's eyes lit up. "Ooh!" she said. "Biology is my favorite subject."

"Anyway," Mrs. P went on, "one of your jobs is to help open mail and packages and log in all the donations. We need to keep very clear records of who gave us what." She frowned slightly. "People can get very touchy when they're not credited properly."

Mrs. P shook her head. "But we're not going to have any problems this year," she went on. "I know you two will help make this auction our most successful ever."

"Of course we will!" I said enthusiastically. I turned to Becky. She nodded. She looked a little pale.

"We're a bit behind, and there's already a stack of unopened packages and mail over on the table in the other room," Mrs. Pritchard finished. She held out some sheets of paper. "You just enter all the information onto these forms, and put any items that arrive onto the table. When you open the boxes, try not to remove any packing material or Bubble Wrap—the items will be safer if they're left in their original packing. Then return the forms to me or to Joan at the end of every day so we can check them."

Becky and I left Mrs. Pritchard's office and got to work right away.

"If one of us does the unpacking and the other one writes everything down, it might be easier to keep track of stuff," I told her.

Becky nodded. "Can I just do the writing?" she asked. "I mean, there might be some expensive stuff in those boxes." She gestured toward the table. "I don't want to mess up."

I nodded and smiled. "Sure," I said. "I don't mind."

For the next two hours I unpacked and opened

mail and Becky wrote down what everyone had sent in. Mostly, people had sent letters offering things like theater tickets, dinners, or services. For instance, Natalie Pittman's mom, who is a lawyer, offered two hours of free legal advice. For each of the letters, all we had to do was write down what the item was and who had donated it and file the letter away in the right place.

But a few people had actually sent in things. I opened one box that had a beautiful turquoise necklace inside. After we listed it, I put it back in the box with a label on it and placed it on the table.

When we'd been working for a little while, Becky and I started to talk a bit. She's really sweet. And it was clear that the job meant a lot to her.

"I know everybody thinks I'm a klutz," she said. "I really appreciate that Mrs. Pritchard gave me this job. Lots of girls think I won't be able to handle it. . . ."

I knew exactly which girls she meant.

Becky gave a small shake of her head. "I just want to prove to them that they're wrong," she finished.

"I know you'll do fine," I told her.

"Of course you will!" a voice echoed.

Becky and I turned. And there, standing right behind us, was Dana, looking perfect, as usual, without a hair out of place. She stared at us.

"Dana," I said. "What are you doing here?"

"I just wanted to see how you two were getting along," she said innocently. "How's it going so far?" She turned and stared at Becky.

Becky lowered her head and looked down at the pages of notes she was working on.

"Things are great," I said.

Dana reached over and took a couple of pages out of Becky's hands. She glanced at them. "Is this the stuff for the auction?" she asked.

"Yes," I said.

Dana took the sheets over to a window and studied them, her back to us. "Wow. A trip to Paris!" she said. "Kristin's parents give really great stuff, don't they?"

I got up, went over to Dana, and took the papers out of her hands. "Sorry, Dana, but we have to get back to work," I said firmly.

Dana shrugged. "Sure. See you," she said. Becky and I watched as she walked away.

Just as she reached the office door, Dana turned around.

"If you need any help," she said, staring at Becky again, "I'd be happy to take over for you . . . I mean, lend a hand." Then she turned and left the office.

I handed the forms back to Becky. "Don't pay

any attention to her," I said. "Let's just finish up here."

When we finished logging all the donations, we went into Mrs. Pritchard's office to give her the completed forms. She riffled through them. "Where's page three, girls?" she asked, looking up at us and handing them back to me.

I looked through them. There were pages one, two, four, and five. But there was no page three.

I looked over at Becky.

She had a totally panicked expression on her face. "I don't know, Mrs. Pritchard," she said breathlessly. "I'm sure it was there before—"

"Well, you'll either have to find the missing page or do it over," Mrs. Pritchard said, frowning slightly. "You know, girls, you're both going to have to be a little more careful. There are hundreds of items coming in for the auction, and we have to keep track of all of them."

Becky stood up straighter and took a deep breath. "It wasn't Ashley's fault," she said. "She was handling the packages. I was writing things down."

Mrs. Pritchard looked over at Becky. "Thank you for telling me that," she said quietly. "But, Becky, you know my 'three strikes and you're out' rule. I need you girls to be totally organized and reliable."

"We'll redo the page," I said quickly. "Don't worry, Mrs. Pritchard."

Mrs. Pritchard nodded. "I'm not worried. I'm sure you girls will handle it. Now"—she looked at her watch— "it's after five-thirty. Isn't it time for you to be heading over to the dining hall for dinner?"

Becky and I left the office. "I think I'll just go straight over!" I told her. "I'm pretty hungry. Are you coming?"

"I'm going back to my room," Becky said. She looked pretty upset. "I don't feel like eating right now."

"Becky, don't worry about that lost page," I told her. "It's not a big deal."

"Yeah, I know," Becky said. "I just don't want to mess up." She looked at me with a little smile. "I really like working with you, Ashley," she said. "And this job means a lot to me."

"You're not going to mess up," I told her. But Becky just shook her head gloomily and turned to leave.

As she headed back to her room, I stared after her. I suddenly realized that I wanted Becky to do well. She was really sweet.

But Becky had a point. Mrs. Pritchard has really

high standards for the girls who work in her office. If Becky made too many mistakes . . . well, Mrs. Pritchard might decide to choose another girl to work in the office.

I'd just have to make sure that didn't happen!

Chapter 3

Wednesday

Dear Diary,

Yesterday afternoon at Starbright Stables, I began to understand why Sean and his parents were so glad to have me helping out with Rigel.

Rigel is a total pain in the neck!

It's not that he's mean or anything. In fact, he's sort of sweet. He just has a very well-developed sense of humor—for a horse.

Taking care of him is like taking care of a really difficult three-year-old kid. The difference is, three-year-olds don't weigh a couple thousand pounds!

After I dropped my stuff off in the tack room, I tried to get him out of his stall so I could muck it out. That means cleaning up the dirty straw, Diary, and making a new bed of nice clean straw for your horse.

I tied a rope to Rigel's halter and tried to lead him out of the stall so I could get to work. But he just planted his feet and wouldn't budge.

This went on for about twenty minutes. I kept pulling and pulling, and he just stood there, leaning back, staring at me with a mulish expression on his face.

Then, just as I was pulling my hardest, Rigel decided to give up and walk forward. I was still pulling, of course, so I flew backward and landed on my rear end on the other side of the barn.

Sean happened to be passing at that moment. "Need any help?" he asked.

"No," I said grimly. "I can handle it."

I tied Rigel up and mucked out his stall. After I finished, I walked him over to the tack room so I could saddle him up.

Getting him over to the tack room was easy enough, but when I tried to open his mouth to put in the bridle, he clamped his teeth together. Even jamming my thumb into the corner of his mouth didn't do anything.

After a long time he finally opened his mouth, so I could get the bit between his teeth. *Then* he started tossing his head around, so it was really hard to buckle the bridle. This horse just does whatever he wants all the time!

After finally finishing with the bridle, I tried to put Rigel's saddle on. But that wasn't any easier. First, he kept walking around in circles when I tried to toss the saddle pad on his back. He did the same thing when I tried to put on his saddle.

Then, when I started to tighten the girth—that's

the strap that goes around his belly—he blew himself up like a balloon. Horses often do that; they swallow lots of air so when they let it out, the saddle hangs loosely on them. This can be dangerous for a rider—if you get on a horse with a saddle that has a loose girth, the saddle can easily slip off him when you're riding. So I had to walk him around a lot and keep tightening the girth till it was right.

When I finally finished, I led him over to the mounting block and got on. Then I tried to get him to move.

Fat chance.

No matter how much I applied pressure with my legs—the signal to tell a horse to go—he just stood there, chewing on his bit.

He is the most difficult horse I've ever met!

I know I'm not a championship rider or anything, so at first, I thought it was all my fault. But Sean says Rigel acts this way with everyone.

If Courtney were working with me, maybe it would be easier. Maybe between the two of us, we could get Rigel to behave. But I've been to the stables three times already, and Courtney hasn't shown up once!

"I don't want to be a pain or a nag or anything," I complained to Campbell and Summer as we hung out in my room last night. "But I need Courtney to work with me! The first day she said she wasn't feeling well. Then she said she had too much homework. Today I couldn't even find her."

Campbell raised her eyebrows. "I saw her in gym just a few hours ago," she said.

I grabbed my pillow and stuck it behind my head. "I'm about to give up. I'm beginning to think she doesn't want to work with me."

"I'm sure that isn't true," Campbell said sympathetically. "I wish you were working at the animal shelter with me, Mary-Kate. All the animals are great. There's this beautiful Dalmatian . . . a family has been in a few times to see him, and I'm hoping they'll adopt him."

"Well, I'd trade places with you any day," Summer said. "The poor animals that come in to see us! Some of them are so sick and scared—"

"But they're there so the vet can make them better," I reminded her.

"I know!" Summer wailed. "But it just breaks my heart to see them like that! I'm so glad Madison is there to help, too," she went on with a little sniff.

"I'm glad you have a great partner," I said, a little sadly.

Campbell turned back to me. "So what are you

going to do about your missing partner?" she asked.

"I don't know," I said, and sighed. "I don't want to talk to Ms. Lewis about Courtney." My friends nodded. No girl in White Oak Academy ever told on another.

"But I have to write the paper with her," I went on. "Plus, I could really use her help. Most of my time is spent just trying to make Rigel move. I barely have time to write up my notes or anything."

"You've got to talk to her, Mary-Kate," Campbell said. "You can't let her keep getting away with this."

I knew Campbell was right. I had to confront Courtney and find out what was going on . . . or my dream assignment was going to turn into a total nightmare!

Dear Diary,

Last night, Phoebe and I were sitting in our room doing some homework and waiting for the pizza to arrive.

"I hope it gets here soon," Phoebe said, chewing on her pencil. "I'm starving!"

Suddenly, there was a knock on the door.

"Maybe the pizza's here!" I said, going to open it.

But it wasn't somebody telling us about the pizza delivery. It was Mrs. Pritchard, and she did not look happy. "Ashley?" she said. "Could you please come with me?"

My heart sank. What was going on?

As I left, I looked over my shoulder at Phoebe. "What's up?" she mouthed.

I shrugged my shoulders. She gave me a good-luck, fingers-crossed sign.

I followed Mrs. Pritchard down the hall until we reached Becky's room. Mrs. Pritchard knocked.

Becky opened the door.

"Becky?" Mrs. Pritchard said. "I need to talk to you and Ashley. Would you come out here and close the door, please?"

Becky nodded and shut the door behind her.

Mrs. Pritchard walked us to the end of the hall and waited until a few girls passed by. "What time is it, girls?" she asked quietly.

I looked over at the hall clock. "Seven forty-five," I said.

"And what do we always get at seven-thirty on Tuesday?" Mrs. Pritchard went on.

"The pizza," I began to say. Then I looked over at Becky.

She looked totally bewildered. "But I called in

the order!" she blurted out. "I did it as soon as I got to the office this afternoon!"

I looked at Becky, and then at Mrs. Pritchard. "Maybe Mario's made a mistake," I said. "Have you called them, Mrs. Pritchard?"

"Yes, I did," Mrs. Pritchard said quietly. "There was no pizza order for White Oak. I spoke to Mario himself. He was very surprised. He knows we place a large order every Tuesday."

Becky looked totally miserable. "I know I called the order in!" she said. "I don't know what could have gone wrong. I'm so sorry."

Mrs. Pritchard shook her head. "I'm sure you are, Becky," she said. "But be more careful the next time, okay? Pizza at White Oak Academy is a long-standing tradition. Now, I have to see what the dining hall can pull together quickly."

Becky nodded miserably. Mrs. Pritchard turned and walked down the hall.

Becky turned to me. "I don't know what happened, Ashley," she said. "I'm sure I called! I wrote down everything in my pocket diary—the phone number and how much to order. But then I couldn't find my diary. So I wrote about a zillion notes to remind myself."

I nodded. "I don't want to see you get into trouble,

Becky," I said. "If you remember calling, I'm sure you did. Something weird must have happened. Maybe there was some kind of mistake at Mario's."

"What. No pizza?"

Becky and I turned around. Standing there were Dana and a few of her friends.

Dana gave Becky a mean little smile.

"Not tonight," I said quickly. "There was just a little mix-up in the pizza delivery."

"Oh, too bad." Dana smiled unpleasantly. "The pizza dinner has been a tradition here for so long." And she turned and walked back down the hall, followed by her friends.

"Funny," I said, staring after Dana, "how Dana is always popping up wherever there's trouble." Could she have done something to mess up the pizza delivery? And she *had* been in the office the day Becky lost the auction form. Could she somehow have taken it?

Could Dana be the cause of Becky's "mistakes"? Did she want Becky's job that badly?

I wondered about Dana all the way back to my room. Then I had to stop wondering about her. I had way too much homework to do . . . and a math test to study for!

I studied for the rest of the evening, and I'm pretty

sure I aced the test today. After it was over, I went down to Mrs. Pritchard's office. Becky was already there, rubbing Tasha behind the ears. The cat was purring loudly.

Mrs. Pritchard had left on a fund-raising trip that morning. She wouldn't be back until next Thursday. We wanted to have everything all organized when she came back. So we got right to work.

This time Becky opened packages while I did the forms. She was worried about making another mistake.

After doing about ten envelopes, Becky held up a package that was about the size of a shoe box, wrapped in brown paper. "I wonder what this is," she said as she began to tear off the tape. She crumpled the brown paper and tossed it on the ground for Tasha to play with. The cat batted it around the floor. Then Becky lifted off the lid of the box and took something out that was wrapped in Bubble Wrap.

"What is it?" I asked.

"I don't know," Becky said. She started to pull the Bubble Wrap off.

Then she giggled. "Wait till you see this!" she said. She reached into the Bubble Wrap like a magician pulling a white rabbit out of a hat.

But what Becky pulled out of the wrapping was not a rabbit. It was the ugliest thing I'd ever seen! "*What* is *that*?" I gasped.

"I don't have a clue," Becky said.

Becky was holding a china statue of a pug dog with a smushed-in face. It wore a collar with a star on it, and a tag that said: CHAMPION STAR: A BLUE RIBBON WINNER.

"I can't even imagine a person who'd want to bid on that thing," I said.

"Yeah. Champion Star is pretty hideous," Becky agreed, grinning.

"Well, we'd better write it up, anyway," I said, picking up my pen. "Someone may want to give it a home."

Becky nodded. "Poor baby," she said, patting the statue on its mustard-brown head. Then she put the statue on the table and rummaged around in the box. She came up with a small card. "It's from a Mrs. Doris Kimberley," she said, handing the card to me.

Just then, Tasha decided she was bored with batting the brown paper ball around the office. She yawned, stretched, and hopped up onto the table.

"Shoo, Tasha!" Becky said, reaching over to shoo the cat away.

Tasha meowed, darted away from Becky, and jumped off the table. Becky's hand accidentally knocked into the ugly pug statue.

Champion Star swayed back and forth as if it were moving in slow motion.

Becky reached over to grab it—but she missed.

We both watched, horrified, as the statue fell off the table.

Becky put her hand over her mouth. Her eyes were wide and frightened. "I can't look!" she gasped. "Is it broken?

I looked down.

The head of Champion Star had broken off the statue, right above the dog's collar.

I picked up both pieces. "It was an accident," I began. "If it was anyone's fault, it was Tasha's."

"But I'll be blamed!" Becky wailed. Her eyes filled with tears. "Mrs. Pritchard told us not to take the Bubble Wrap off. And I forgot. I'm always doing something wrong! And I so wanted this to be different. . . ."

"Becky, you're not always doing something wrong," I began. "Anyway, we're both responsible for doing this job, so we're both responsible for the statue."

Becky turned to me. "Ashley, please," she said.

"Help me! If Mrs. Pritchard gets mad and fires me, it'll just prove to Dana and everybody else that I'm hopeless!"

I knew Becky was right. Dana could be really mean.

But I couldn't magically put Champion Star back together again.

What could I possibly do to help?

Chapter 4

Friday

Dear Diary,

Right now, I'm sitting in my room, staring at the two pieces of Mrs. Doris Kimberley's ugly pug and wondering how I got myself into this mess.

After the statue broke on Wednesday, Becky put the two pieces of Champion Star back into the box and shoved it into my arms. "You've got to hide this," she said.

"I can't do that," I began.

"Please!" Becky looked at me desperately. "Just give me a little time to figure out what to do. I can't take it. If Lily finds this—"

Lily was Becky's roommate. She was also the daughter of Cecilia Vanderhoff, the head of the Board of Trustees. I could see why Becky wouldn't want Lily anywhere near that box.

"Please!" Becky said again. "Mrs. Pritchard isn't coming back to the office until next week. I can't tell her until she's back from her trip, anyway. I just don't want Joan or anybody else to find it!"

I shook my head. But she was so upset, and I felt so sorry for her, Diary, that I took the box.

Now I'm stuck with it.

I stared at the broken statue, feeling pretty guilty myself. I never should have agreed to keep it in my room. It was true that there wasn't much we could do until Mrs. Pritchard came back, but maybe we should have told Joan. . . .

Suddenly, somebody knocked on the door.

I quickly shoved the two pieces of Champion Star back into the box. The box was halfway under my bed when Dana poked her head inside my room!

"Ashley!" she said, smiling. "Your door was open." She looked down at the box. "What's in there?" she asked.

"Uh . . . nothing," I said. "A care package from my dad."

Dana nodded. "That's nice," she said, staring closely at me.

"So . . . uh . . . why are you here?" I asked.

"I just came to say hi," Dana said. She walked over to my desk and perched on the chair.

"That's nice," I said. I didn't believe her, of course. Dana had never come over to say hi to me before.

I was right. "And I just wanted to tell you something," Dana added. She opened her green eyes wide. "Poor Becky," she began. "I mean, she must be overwhelmed! She's never been . . . well, a very put-together kind of person, you know?"

I shook my head. "No, I don't," I said. "I think she's really nice."

"Well . . . nice, sure," Dana said. When she said the word "nice," it looked like she was chewing on a lemon. "But I just wanted you to know, if Becky isn't up to the job . . . well, I'll be happy to take over for her. You know, when my mother went to White Oak Academy, she was one of the headmistress's assistants. My grandmother had the same job when *she* was here. They've told me a million stories!"

Just then, we heard a jumble of voices from the hallway.

I jumped up to open the door and see what was going on.

A lot of kids were racing down the hall.

"C'mon, Ashley!" Mary-Kate called cheerily. "There's pizza tonight . . . to make up for Tuesday!"

I really wanted to follow Mary-Kate and ask her advice about the ugly pug over a slice of pizza. But Becky had sworn me to secrecy.

Instead, I turned back to Dana. She was reaching for the box under the bed.

"The pizza isn't under my bed, Dana," I said coldly. "What are you doing?"

Dana just looked at me. Before I could say another word, she got up and walked past me out the door. I closed the door behind me and followed her down the hall to the common room.

Had Dana opened the box?

Would she tell Mrs. Pritchard about the broken pug?

Working at the job in Mrs. Pritchard's office was supposed to be fun. But, somehow, in one short week, it had turned into a big mess.

And it didn't seem like there was much that I could do about it. . . .

Dear Diary,

"Rigel! Pick up your foot!" I pleaded.

It was Friday afternoon. Rigel was in his stall and I was standing next to him, tugging at his right front leg. Sean had asked me to check for any pebbles or rocks that might have gotten stuck in Rigel's shoe. He thought Rigel had been favoring that foot the other day.

Rigel just stood there, staring down at me.

Then he grabbed my baseball cap again.

I reached up for it, but Rigel raised his head and waved my cap as if it were a flag. Then he dropped it in the corner of the stall.

I sighed. Stealing my cap had become Rigel's favorite trick.

I reached over and picked it up, brushing the straw off. Luckily, the straw was clean. I had just finished mucking out Rigel's stall. I started to put the cap back on my head, but then I changed my mind. I jammed it into my back pocket instead. "You wait here," I told Rigel. "I'm going to find Sean and see if he can help."

I left the stall and walked toward the barn doors. And guess who I saw there?

Courtney! She didn't look like she was dressed for stable work. In fact, she was wearing a pleated miniskirt and a pair of short boots that my sister Ashley would have loved. "I'm sorry, Mary-Kate," she said, looking pretty embarrassed. "I know I've missed a few days. . . ."

"That's okay," I said. "I'm just happy you're here now. Do you know anything about horses?"

She nodded. "A little," she said.

"Okay. Do you have any idea how to get a horse to pick up his feet when he doesn't want to? 'Cause I sure don't."

Courtney smiled. "It can be hard sometimes," she said. "You know how you hold his leg, just above the ankle?"

I nodded.

"Well, have you tried squeezing your thumb and first finger together? That usually does the trick. And don't forget to keep asking him to pick his leg up."

I looked at her, surprised. "You sound like you know a lot more than a little about horses," I said.

I started walking back to Rigel's stall, and Courtney followed me. "Rigel's a great horse," I told her as we walked. "He just likes messing with me. I'm really glad you're here. With two of us working with him, he won't be able to get away with as much. Plus, we have to start talking about our paper. . . ."

When we got to the stall door, Rigel stuck his head out. Courtney reached tentatively and touched his nose. "You're a pretty boy, aren't you?" she said softly.

Rigel perked up his ears and nuzzled her hand. She scratched him behind the ears.

He looked blissful.

"You've put him in a good mood," I whispered. "Come on, maybe we can get him to raise that leg. . . ."

Rigel snorted, and Courtney backed away.

"Uh, Mary-Kate?" she said. "I only came here to

tell you I have to do something this afternoon. I'll meet you here on Monday after school. I promise this time!"

And before I could say anything, she fled down to the end of the barn and disappeared out the door.

I stared after her. Had I said something wrong? What was *with* Courtney?

Just then, Sean came out of the tack room. "Was that the famous Courtney?" he asked, gesturing after her.

"Yup," I told him.

He shrugged. "Easy come, easy go, huh?"

"You can say that again!" I told him. "Sean, do you have a second? I've just got to get Rigel to pick up his feet."

Sean helped me clean Rigel's hooves. Then I curried Rigel—that means brushing him with a stiff wire brush to clean his coat—and fed him.

I went into the tack room, where I had left my backpack. I pulled out my notebook and wrote down what I had done at the stables that day and how Rigel had behaved. I've been taking a lot of notes for the paper. I wrote about what I was doing to care for Rigel and how he acted. I even wrote about his game of taking my baseball cap!

I had already started on the outline, too. I figured

I couldn't wait for Courtney's help. She clearly had no intention of working with me. It was starting to look like I was going to have to do this assignment all on my own.

The whole thing was totally unfair!

Chapter 5

Monday

Dear Diary,

This weekend, Becky and I went to the mall.

But it wasn't to go clothes shopping.

"I want to try to find a statue of a pug dog to replace the one I broke," she told me.

"It wasn't your fault," I began. But Becky wasn't listening.

"If we can find one just like it, then maybe Mrs. Pritchard won't be so mad," she said eagerly. She patted her backpack. "I have thirty-five dollars and fifty-three cents in here," she added, "and I'll spend every bit of it if I have to."

I shook my head. "Becky, you'll never find the same kind of dog," I began.

"But I have to try!" Becky looked determined. "If you don't want to go with me, Ashley, I'll understand. It wasn't your fault that it broke."

"Of course I'll go with you," I told her.

We went to three different department stores and a gazillion boutiques that had little gifty things. Actually, there were more dog statues than I had expected; people must love collecting them.

But by late afternoon, we hadn't found anything close to the ugly pug.

Becky looked around in despair. "There!" she said, pointing to another store. "That one. Maybe there's something in there."

I sighed as I followed Becky into the store.

We rummaged around, looking at lamps and copies of old paintings and dishes and . . . wait a minute. What was that?

I walked over to a shelf and moved a collection of frames aside.

There was a statue of a pug dog. It actually looked a lot like the one that was broken.

"Did you find anything?" Becky asked, coming up beside me.

"No," I said, shaking my head. "I thought that one might be . . . but he's standing, not sitting. And he doesn't have that little star on his collar."

Becky's face fell.

"Look, Becky," I said gently, "I don't think we're going to be able to replace the dog. We're going to have to tell Mrs. Pritchard the truth when she comes back on Thursday. She'll know what to do."

Becky looked at me and shook her head sadly. "I know that, Ashley," she said. "And thanks for helping."

"I still say it wasn't really your fault," I told her.

Becky's face fell. "But Mrs. Pritchard won't believe that," she said. "She knows I'm a klutz. I'll lose my job for sure," she said. She looked at me hopefully. "Maybe we can repair the dog." She looked around. "I bet there's a place we can buy Super-Duper Glue around here somewhere. That stuff can glue anything back together."

I shook my head. "It'll never work."

Becky grabbed me by the arm. "What do I have to lose?" she said. "The dog is already broken."

So I gave in, Diary. We went back to my room and we tried to Super-Duper Glue the dog's head back onto its body.

The glue was incredibly sticky. Becky got it all over her hands, and it dripped onto her plaid skirt as she spread a bead of it around the head of the dog.

Suddenly, there was a knock on the door. "Is anybody there?"

It was Dana.

What was it with Dana? Does she have X-ray vision? Why is she always around when things are going wrong?

Just then, Becky screamed, "Oh, no!"

I turned around to see what had happened.

Becky was tugging at the dog's head. She had

dropped it into her lap—and now, it was glued to her skirt!

Dear Diary,

This afternoon, just as I was about to head over to the stables, guess who came to my room? Courtney!

"Do you want to walk over to Starbright together?" she asked.

"Yeah, sure!" I told her. *Finally*, I thought.

Things seemed pretty okay on the way over. We talked about Ms. Lewis, and about our other classes. Courtney really seems to love White Oak.

Then I told her some more about Rigel.

"He's quite a handful, isn't he?" Courtney said, giggling.

"A few handfuls, I'd say," I told her. "At least there's a lot to write about! I've been taking tons of notes, and I've been working on our outline."

Courtney looked guilty. "Gee. I didn't realize you had done that much already," she said. "Thanks a lot. I promise I'll do more of the work when we write up the paper."

I smiled. "That would be terrific," I said.

Courtney and I were getting along great. Things were going to be okay after all.

When we got to the stables, Courtney turned to me. "Mary-Kate?" she said. "I just have to go to the bathroom. I'll meet you back at Rigel's stall in a few minutes."

"Sure," I said. "I was going to muck out his stall, and then take him out for a walk. I'll see you back there."

I thought things were fine.

But Courtney didn't show up.

How long could she be in the bathroom? I wondered. *Could there be something wrong?* So after I got Rigel out of his stall, I tied him up and went to check on her.

But the bathroom was empty.

Then I searched the entire barn.

I found her in the tack room. She was polishing a saddle.

"Courtney?" I said.

She glanced up at me. "Hey, Mary-Kate!" she said. "I ran into Sean, and he asked me if I could clean up a little around here. . . ."

"Oh," I said, a little annoyed that she had left me to do all the dirty work. *At least she's doing something*, I told myself. But she wasn't working on our assignment.

"Courtney," I asked, "is everything okay? I

mean, is there a problem with me or something? I thought you were going to help me with Rigel."

Courtney shook her head until her brown hair flew around her head. "No . . . no problem at all!" she said. "I'll be done in a sec."

I stood there for a minute. Then I nodded. "Okay. I'm going to exercise Rigel now . . . *if* he decides to move. I'll see you in the ring."

Courtney nodded. "I'll be there right away," she promised.

I went back to Rigel. I managed to saddle and bridle him. Then I led him over to the ring, where Sean was exercising one of the other horses.

I got up on Rigel. As usual, he just sat there. I must have looked like an idiot trying to make him take a step. Sean looked over and gave me a sympathetic smile.

Finally, Rigel decided to move. He walked around the ring. Then he started to trot. Of course, I hadn't asked him to. Then he began to canter, which is like a slow gallop.

I should have stopped him—I hadn't asked for a canter, either. But his canter was really nice and smooth.

Just as I was starting to enjoy myself, he stopped dead, almost throwing me over his head. I grabbed for his neck and just barely managed to stay on.

"Rigel, what do you have against me?" I groaned, sitting up in the saddle again.

Rigel flicked his ears back. Then he turned around and looked at me. I could swear that he gave me a wink.

I got off and walked him around to cool him down a bit. I kept walking him, waiting for Courtney to show up.

She never did.

So I took Rigel back to his stall.

On the way, I passed the tack room.

Courtney wasn't there.

I took the saddle and bridle off Rigel and brushed him until his coat gleamed.

Then I hung everything up in the tack room and went to look for Courtney again.

I looked all around the barn. This time, she was nowhere to be found.

I walked slowly back to school, wondering about Courtney.

Everything had seemed to be okay for a little while. We seemed to be getting along fine.

So what had happened? Why had she disappeared?

Was I going to have to do the whole project

alone? Was Courtney going to get a grade based on my hard work?

I turned into the White Oak gates and headed for my dorm.

It just wasn't fair! Ms. Lewis had given us both the assignment. I shouldn't have to do it all by myself!

But, besides telling on Courtney, what else could I do?

Chapter 6

Tuesday

Dear Diary,

So there we were: Dana knocking on my door, and Becky sitting on my bed and tugging on Champion Star's head, which was stuck to her skirt. She looked as if she wanted to disappear.

I went over to her and tried to help her get it off. "I don't want to tear your skirt," I muttered, trying to scrape the glue off with my nails.

"Is something wrong?" Dana called through the door. "I can go and get a teacher."

"No, no!" I called cheerfully. "I'm . . . that is, we're just in the middle of a slightly, uh, sticky situation."

"Can I come in?"

I looked at Becky, who shook her head violently. But I knew if I didn't let Dana in, it would look really strange.

"Cover it up!" I whispered, grabbing a pillow from Phoebe's bed and tossing it to Becky. She plopped the pillow onto her lap and put both elbows on the pillow.

Then I opened the door. "What's up?" I asked Dana, standing right in the doorway.

Dana pushed past me. She looked over at Becky and nodded. Then her eyes scanned my room. It was almost as if she was looking for something.

"What are you doing here?" I asked her, stepping between her and Becky.

"Oh," Dana said. She reached into her bag and brought out a small notebook. "I was actually looking for Becky. I wanted to return this."

She held out the notebook. Becky reached for it, but Dana didn't move.

And Becky, of course, couldn't get up. She had a dog's head stuck to her skirt under Phoebe's pillow.

I reached over and took the notebook out of Dana's hand and brought it over to the bed. "Is it yours?" I asked Becky.

Becky took it from me, keeping her other hand on the pillow in her lap. She struggled to open it with one hand. Then she nodded. "Yes," she said. "It's mine."

"Oh, good!" Dana said. "I thought it might be. I didn't see a name on it. But there was a note inside about the pizza delivery—" She stopped suddenly. "Oh. That's why you forgot to order the pizza, isn't it?" she said. "You lost your diary!"

Becky's face flushed. "I didn't forget!" she cried.

"Whatever," Dana said. She walked toward the

door, waved a hand, and disappeared again.

I shut the door after her and turned to Becky.

"She probably read the whole thing," Becky wailed. "And it has all sorts of personal stuff in it!"

"Nothing you can do about it now," I said. "Anyway, we have bigger problems. Let's see if we can get that dog off your skirt!"

I sat down next to Becky. She held the dog while I tried to peel little bits of glue off the dog and her skirt. The glue got stuck in my nails, and bits of it went all over my bed. But, finally, the dog's head pulled free of Becky's skirt. I was glad we weren't using one of those really permanent glues—it never would've come off!

I stared at Becky's skirt. "Your skirt will never be the same!"

Becky shrugged. "My mom is used to my spilling stuff all over myself," she said. Then she pointed at my broken nails. "You *so* need a manicure!"

We both laughed. My nails were a chipped mess.

Then I took the body of the dog out of the box and, together, Becky and I carefully glued the two pieces together.

I held them in place so the glue would set. "You know," I said, looking at it critically, "it doesn't look that terrible. The break was just under the collar.

You can hardly see it." I turned to Becky. "But that doesn't change things."

Becky sighed. "I know, Ashley," she said. "I know I have to tell Mrs. Pritchard."

"I'm going to take this back to the office," I said. "We'll leave it there until Mrs. Pritchard gets back. I'm sure she won't be angry at you. After all, it was mostly Tasha's fault!"

Becky eyes filled with tears. "I hope you're right," she said. "But I don't think she'll blame her cat. I think she'll blame me."

Dear Diary,

Well, Diary, I finally figured what to do about Courtney.

What helped me make up my mind? Talking to Ashley, of course.

"I don't know what's going on," I said to my sister after dinner on Monday. "Courtney seems nice enough. But I've been on the project for almost two weeks now, and she's barely shown up! And even then, she didn't stick around."

"Have you spoken to her about it?" my sister asked me.

"Not really," I admitted. "I feel weird about accusing her of, well, being lazy. Maybe it's that she hates me and doesn't want to spend any time with me!"

"Nobody hates you, Mary-Kate," Ashley said. "How could they? You're my sister!" She smiled.

I smiled back. But then I shook my head. "I can't go talk to Ms. Lewis, can I?" I said. "That would be telling. I just don't know what to do!"

"Yes, you do," Ashley said gently. "You just don't want to do it."

I sat there, staring at my sneakers. "Yeah," I said finally. "I do know. I need to have a talk with Courtney. I can't let her get away with not doing the assignment. I have to tell her that if she doesn't start coming to the stables and helping out, I'm going to have to tell Ms. Lewis."

"Sounds like a plan to me," Ashley said.

I clearly wasn't going to find Courtney at Starbright Stables, so after classes today, I went straight to her room.

She looked shocked to see me when she opened the door. "Uh, Mary-Kate!" she said. "What's up? Are you going to the stables today?"

"No," I said. "And neither are you, Courtney. In fact, you're never going to the stables, are you?"

Courtney stuck her chin out. "I was there the other day," she said. "I polished saddles until my fingers were numb!"

I stared at her. "You've hardly even met Rigel," I said calmly. "Courtney, we've got to talk."

Courtney looked down.

"Can I come in?" I asked.

Without a word, she stood aside.

I walked into her room and turned to face her. "What's going on, Courtney?" I asked. "You've only been to the stables twice in almost two whole weeks. The first time you left right away. And yesterday you spent the entire time in the tack room, hiding out. Are you hiding from me?"

"Of course not!" Courtney burst out.

"Well, it sure seems that way," I told her. "We're supposed to be doing this paper together. I know you said you'd write a lot of it, but how can you when you haven't worked with Rigel at all? Besides, I really need your help with him. I can't do it by myself. I keep having to ask Sean for help."

Courtney hung her head. "I'd like to help you," she said in a small voice. "But . . ."

"But what?"

"I'm . . . I'm afraid of horses," Courtney whispered.

Suddenly, I felt terrible. Poor Courtney! And here I was, pushing her. I should have realized!

"Courtney! Why didn't you tell me?" I said.

"Maybe I can do something to make it easier for you. Horses are great! You just have to know how to act around them, how to treat them. I know just a little . . . but I can help. I know I can."

Courtney looked up at me. There was so much pain in her eyes, I was shocked. "It's not that," she said. "I know all that stuff! That's not the problem! And there's nothing anybody can do to help me. Nothing at all!"

And without another word, she burst into tears and raced out of her room and down the hall.

I just stood there. What had I done? What did Courtney mean? Why was she crying?

What was going on?

Chapter 7

Wednesday

Dear Diary,

Boy, do I have a lot to report!

You know how I told you all about what happened when I went to talk to Courtney?

Well, even more stuff happened after that . . . and it explains everything!

After Courtney ran out of her room, I ran after her. I wandered around for a while, looking everywhere I could think of. But she had totally disappeared.

So I went back to my room. I stormed inside and slammed the door behind me.

Campbell was there, sitting at her desk.

"You're not going to believe it," I told her. I flopped down on my bed and pushed my hair out of my eyes.

Campbell gestured toward the corner of our room.

I blinked.

Sitting right there, on our beanbag chair, was Courtney.

I jumped off the bed. "Courtney!" I cried. "Are you okay? I was so worried!"

Courtney nodded shakily.

"Yeah," she said. "I'm sorry, Mary-Kate. I've been walking all over campus. I know I've been a real pain. I want to tell you the truth."

"I have to go to the library," Campbell said quickly, hopping up from her desk and grabbing a book. "Great seeing you, Courtney."

Courtney gave Campbell a weak smile, and Campbell left the room, closing the door gently behind her.

"I used to be a pretty good rider," Courtney finally said. She didn't look at me—her eyes were focused on the wall. "I grew up around horses, back in Kentucky. I love horses. My parents have had a horse farm ever since I was, oh, two."

She smiled sadly. "You should see the pictures my folks have of me. I was so tiny, and the horses were so big. But I wasn't afraid of them at all. My dad used to say that I seemed to be able to 'talk horse'. . . ." Her voice trailed off, and she took a shaky breath.

"But last July," Courtney went on, "I was riding one of my parents' horses, Blue Fire, in a gymkhana—that's a kind of jumping competition. And I got thrown." She held up her right arm. "I broke my wrist in two places," she said.

"I'm so sorry," I said. "I didn't know—"

Courtney held up her hand. "Of course you didn't," she said. "I didn't have the guts to tell you." She shook her head. "Anyway, my wrist healed pretty quickly. But the next time I went to get on a horse . . . I just couldn't. I was too terrified to try again."

I could see the pain in Courtney's eyes.

"My instructor told me these things happen," she went on miserably. "That I would get over it. But the rest of the summer went by, and I didn't get over it. I missed horses like crazy, but the minute I got near to riding one, I got the shakes."

I didn't know what to say, so I kept quiet. Soon, Courtney continued.

"So when I heard that I was assigned to Starbright Stables . . . I tried everything I could think of to get out of it." Courtney bit her lip. "Of course, Ms. Lewis wouldn't let me quit . . . even though I begged her. But I couldn't tell her the reason. I was too embarrassed."

I nodded slowly. "I heard you talking to her that day," I told Courtney. "I thought maybe you didn't like me."

"Oh, Mary-Kate!" Courtney said, her eyes bright. "I like you a lot! I think you're great! So does

Ms. Lewis," she added. "Anyway, she said I had to stick to the assignment. So . . ." Courtney's voice trailed off.

"You just didn't show up," I finished for her.

"Yeah." She nodded. She looked up at me. "I'll make it up to you—I can write the whole paper myself. You can tell me everything that goes on with that horse. . . . I'm sure I could do it!"

I shook my head. "No," I said. "That wouldn't be fair, either. We can do the work together from now on. We just have to figure out how. . . ." I sat there, thinking, for a moment.

Then I got an idea. "Look," I told her. "Why don't we both go down to the stables tomorrow? You don't have to ride or anything. But you know a lot more about horses than me. I can be the one who goes near Rigel . . . who cleans up and stuff. And you can help me figure out how to make him behave."

Courtney thought about this for a minute. Then she nodded. "Yeah. I think I could do that."

So that's the plan, Diary. We're both going over to the stables tomorrow, right after school.

The question is . . . will Courtney be able to stick around long enough to help?

Can she really handle it?

Two of a Kind Diaries

Dear Diary,

Things are so messed up! I can't tell Becky—she'll freak out. And I can't even tell my sister—which is what I want to do more than anything in the world.

After I did my homework this afternoon, I decided to deal with my laundry. Laundry pickup is tomorrow, and I needed to make sure there was nothing in my laundry bag that shouldn't go out.

Usually I hate to take care of the laundry—except when I need to think. There's something about sorting through my clothes that helps me focus on a problem.

I pulled the sheets off my bed and crammed them into one laundry bag. Then I dumped my dirty clothes onto my mattress and started going through my pockets.

I found a couple of scrunchies and a dollar bill in one pair of jeans. Then, in another one of my jeans pockets, I felt something else. I pulled it out and looked at it.

It was a plain envelope, addressed to White Oak Academy. At the bottom of the envelope, it said, ATTENTION: AUCTION. But there was no stamp on it.

I frowned. Where had this come from?

The envelope was already open, so I reached in and took out the letter that was inside.

I started to read.

"Dear Mrs. Pritchard," the letter said. "I am delighted to send in my annual donation to the White Oaks school auction. I expect that you'll make a great deal of money auctioning off my little pug statue. I look forward to seeing all of you at the auction."

It was signed "Doris Kimberley."

I stared at the letter. A little pug dog? That must be Champion Star, the statue Tasha had broken! And it sounded like Mrs. Kimberley thought the dog was really valuable!

But where had the letter come from? And why was it in my jeans pocket?

I thought and thought. And then I figured it out.

When the statue had broken, I was holding the letter that came in the box. In all the excitement, I must have stuck it in my pocket and forgotten all about it.

I started to go over to Becky's room to tell her about the letter. But then I stopped.

If the dog was worth a lot of money, there was no way Becky or I would be able to replace it. And if Becky knew it was worth a lot of money, she'd freak out. She'd never want to tell Mrs. Pritchard. And then I'd have to. And then . . .

I felt like screaming.

Should I keep the letter a secret?

What was the right thing to do?

I had absolutely no idea.

Chapter 8

Thursday

Dear Diary,

This morning at breakfast, I found Becky sitting at a table in the cafeteria. She didn't look very hungry.

I sat down next to her.

"Today's the day," I said. "We're going to go into Mrs. Pritchard's office this afternoon and tell her exactly what happened."

Becky nodded. "I know," she said. "I was up all last night thinking about it. I'd like to keep it a secret . . . but it would be wrong."

"I'll explain about Tasha," I told her. "Nobody will blame you—I know it."

Becky sighed. "It's okay," she said sadly. "I just want to get the whole thing over with."

"Great," I said, feeling a little better already. "I'll meet you at Mrs. Pritchard's office after classes."

Becky nodded. "I'll be there," she said.

Right after school, I headed to the office. Becky got there a second later.

I dumped my backpack on the floor and walked over to the table, where I had left the box with the dog in it.

But it wasn't there.

"I know I left it here!" I said, starting to panic. I looked all over the table. But there was no box!

"Is this what you're looking for?"

I looked around.

Dana was standing in the doorway. And in her hands was the box, with the pug dog inside!

"I found this on the table, Ashley," she said, her eyes narrowed. "I was looking for Mrs. Pritchard. It's the same box you had in your room. The one you were trying to hide."

Dana rolled her eyes. "Did you really think you could get away with trying to fix it?" she said. She turned to Becky. "I'm afraid when the headmistress finds out what's been going on, you're *both* going to lose your jobs."

Becky's lip started to tremble.

Dana turned around. "I'm headed over to the dining hall right now to find Mrs. Pritchard," she said. "Joan said she was on her way there. You wanna come?" And without another word, she headed out and down the hall.

Becky stared at me.

"What are we going to do now, Ashley?" She moaned.

I took a deep breath. "Exactly what we planned

to do before," I told her. "Tell the truth. Come on!"

I raced out of the room. Becky was right on my heels.

We headed across campus at a run, and crossed through a gap between buildings to save time.

"I thought we were going to the dining hall—"

We found Mrs. Pritchard at the bottom of the stairs, talking to a few girls.

Dana was nowhere in sight.

As we raced toward Mrs. Pritchard, she began to climb the stairs.

"Mrs. Pritchard! Mrs. Pritchard!" Becky's voice rang out.

I turned in surprise. There was a look of determination on Becky's face. She picked up speed and sprinted up the steps.

Mrs. Pritchard turned around and saw us.

Becky stepped up to her, totally out of breath. "Mrs. Pritchard, we have something to tell you," she gasped. "I'm really sorry—"

"I'm sure you are," a voice said.

The voice belonged to Dana.

She was standing at the top of the stairs, holding the box.

"I think this belongs to the school, Mrs. Pritchard," she said, handing the box over.

Mrs. Pritchard looked from Dana to me to Becky and back again. Then she looked in the box. "What's this all about, girls?" she asked.

Dana opened her mouth to speak, but then Becky stepped forward. "Mrs. Pritchard," Becky said, her voice shaking a little. "Before you went away, there was an accident. Somebody sent in this dog for the auction, and it got broken."

"It wasn't Becky's fault!" I said, jumping in. "Tasha jumped up on the table, and Becky was trying to get her down—"

Mrs. Pritchard stared down at the dog.

"It doesn't look broken," she said.

I hung my head. "We glued it back together," I said in a tiny voice.

"It was my idea," Becky added. "I thought we could fix it. I was going to tell you . . . but then you went away." She hung her head. "And I was scared," she finished sadly.

Mrs. Pritchard kept staring into the box.

For some reason, it looked like her mouth was twitching. Then she looked up at Dana. "And what do you have to do with all of this?"

For the first time, Dana looked a little flustered. "Well, I, uh, found the statue," she said, stumbling over her words. "In your office. But before that I saw it in Ashley's room. Ashley had hidden it there. I thought it might be valuable."

"And what were you doing sneaking around Ashley's room?" Mrs. Pritchard asked sharply.

"I wasn't sneaking!" Dana said. She suddenly looked nervous. "I had overheard Ashley and Becky talking about the dog. I knew it was broken and that they were trying to hide it. When I saw the box in Ashley's room . . . and then I saw it again in your office . . . I just thought you should know about it, that's all," Dana finished.

"Well," Mrs. Pritchard said, looking hard at Dana. "Thank you, Dana." She turned and nodded to Becky and me. "Girls? Would you please come with me?"

Mrs. Pritchard headed off across campus, and we followed.

Dana flashed me a triumphant look as she went back up the stairs of the dining hall.

Mrs. Pritchard didn't say a word all the way to her office. I couldn't see her face, either. It was getting dark.

When we got there, she put the box down on her desk and took off her coat. "So you weren't going to tell me about this," she said, gesturing to the box.

Becky gulped. "I was," she said in a tiny voice.

"But I already had two strikes against me. I knew I'd have to tell you. But I wanted to keep my job so much! I kept thinking there was a way out . . . if we could fix it, or I could replace it. . . ."

She stopped. "But I was wrong," she finally said. "The whole thing was all my fault. Please, please let Ashley keep her job, Mrs. Pritchard. I made her promise not to tell you, and she was just keeping her word."

Mrs. Pritchard turned to me. "What do you have to say for yourself?" she asked.

I hung my head. "I'm sorry," I said. "But I didn't think it was Becky's fault. I just wanted to help her any way I could. She works so hard, Mrs. Pritchard—she really deserves this job."

I took a deep breath and reached into my pocket. "There's one more thing," I said. "This is the letter about the pug dog. It was in the box. I put it in my pocket, then forgot about it until I found it again yesterday. Becky hasn't even seen it yet. I didn't want her to worry, but it looks like the statue could be worth a lot of money."

Becky gasped.

I handed the envelope to Mrs. Pritchard. She opened it and read the letter. She nodded slowly. "It can be hard to tell when you're helping a friend and when you're not," she said slowly. She looked at Becky again. "So now that you've both confessed, what are we going to do about all this?"

Becky gulped. "I can't pay you back right away—but maybe if I get a job on the weekends, I can pay you a little every week."

"We can *both* pay you," I said firmly.

Becky turned to me. "Ashley, it had nothing to do with you!" she cried. "I can't let you pay anything!"

Mrs. Pritchard held up her hands. For some weird reason, she didn't look upset at all. In fact, she looked like she was enjoying herself. "Hold it, hold it," she said. "There's something you girls should know. This statue isn't worth much at all. Oh, I'd say you could replace it for about . . . fifteen dollars."

My jaw dropped. "Fifteen dollars?" I said, dumbfounded.

"Yes," Mrs. Prichard said. She was definitely smiling now. "Mrs. Kimberley likes to think that her donations are worth a lot of money. But she bought her entire collection years ago at the local Stanley Green Emporium. You know, the place that sells all those little statues and things?"

I frowned. "Wasn't that one of the stores we went to in the mall?" I asked Becky.

"I think so," Becky said slowly.

"Anyway, we humor her and put her little dogs in the auction every year," Mrs. Pritchard went on. "They bring about forty or fifty dollars. People are generous.

"Why don't I talk to Mrs. Kimberley?" she went on. "I'm sure you girls can find something to replace her little donation."

I could feel my stomach unclench.

"We'll go to the mall right away!" Becky said eagerly, a big grin on her face. Then the grin faded. "I guess I'm going to lose my job, right, Mrs. Pritchard?" she said.

Mrs. Pritchard frowned.

"I don't mind," Becky went on. "But please, please don't let Ashley go. She was just trying to be nice to me. None of this was her fault."

"I want a little time to think about all of this," Mrs. Pritchard said. "Why don't you girls go off to dinner? I'll tell you my decision in the morning."

Becky nodded.

So now we wait, Diary. Will Becky keep her job? Will I keep mine?

We'll know tomorrow. In the meantime, I don't know how I'm going to get to sleep!

Wish on a Star

Dear Diary,

Diary, it's incredible!

After school yesterday, Courtney and I went over to the stables. Courtney stuck with me the entire way, even if she did stay on the other side of the hall when I took Rigel out of his stall.

The afternoon was crisp and sunny, so we went out to the paddock. Courtney sat on the fence while I tightened the girth on Rigel's saddle and tried to climb on board.

Rigel wasn't going to let me, though.

As I tried to get on him, he started walking around in a circle. I kept trying to get my foot up into the stirrup. But just as my toe touched the metal, he would walk around some more so the stirrup was just out of reach. I followed him around and around, picking my foot up and missing the stirrup until I actually started to get dizzy!

Courtney started to giggle.

"This isn't funny!" I said. "It's exactly the kind of thing he does all the time!"

"You just need to show him who's boss," Courtney said, stifling her laughter. She hopped off the fence and came over to us.

She grabbed Rigel's bridle right under the bit

and whispered something into his nose.

"Easy, boy," she murmured, putting her hand on his shoulder.

Rigel stopped. His ears perked up, and he lowered his head and nudged Courtney in the chest.

"You're a silly baby, aren't you?" she asked. She glanced over at me. "You can get on now," she said.

So I did.

"What's with him, anyway?" she asked, backing away a few feet. Rigel stood there looking at her, ears pricked and head forward.

"He fell while he was jumping a fence," I told her. "He didn't get hurt, but he's been stubborn and hard to control ever since."

Courtney looked up at me. "So he was spooked, too," she said. She turned and climbed back onto the fence.

I was about to press my legs into Rigel's side to tell him to move forward.

He stood there quietly, waiting.

And that's when I got my brilliant idea.

I let my legs hang loose and sat there like I was on the beanbag chair in my room. "Come on, boy," I said. "Come on."

Rigel, of course, didn't move. No horse would have.

Courtney looked at me, frowning.

"This silly horse won't do anything I ask him to do," I said, shrugging my shoulders and trying to look innocent.

Courtney stared at me. I just sat there, asking Rigel to move but doing nothing to make him.

Finally, Courtney couldn't stand it anymore.

"Mary-Kate?" she said. "I don't want to tell you what to do . . ."

"Are you kidding?" I told her. "I need all the help I can get!"

Courtney nodded. "Well," she asked me, "are you using your seat and your legs?"

"What do you mean?" I asked innocently.

"You know," Courtney said. "Sitting forward and using your body. To make Rigel move forward."

"I'm not sure," I said. I crossed my fingers. I sounded like a dope. Would Courtney buy it? "Could you show me?" I asked her.

Courtney hesitated for a second. Then she jumped off the fence and walked over to us again. "You know you have to sit in a certain way and squeeze him with your legs in order to get him to move," she said, looking up at me.

"I do?" I said.

Courtney stared at me. I was afraid for a minute

that she knew what I was doing. *Come on, Courtney*, I thought. *Make me get off the horse. Show me how it's done. . . .*

Courtney took hold of Rigel's reins again. "Can I borrow your helmet?" she said.

"Oh, sure," I said, trying to look calm. Inside, I was thinking, *You go, girl!*

I slipped off of Rigel and took off my helmet. I handed it to Courtney. Then I went to stand by the fence.

Courtney put on my helmet. Then, in one smooth motion—before Rigel could act up—she hopped onto his back. I don't think she totally realized what she was doing.

Rigel stood still for a second. Then his head went up and curved forward, and he stood up straighter. It looked like an electric current was running through him. He looked beautiful.

Courtney didn't seem to do anything at all. But, suddenly, Rigel was walking briskly around the ring as if he were trying to show off for a crowd.

"It's all in how you sit on a horse," she said to me. "How you balance your body. You use your seat even more than your legs . . . like this."

Rigel was suddenly trotting.

Courtney really was incredible. For the next

forty-five minutes, I got a lesson from the best rider I had ever seen.

At one point, Sean walked over to the paddock. He stared at Courtney and Rigel. "Who is that?" he asked me quietly.

"That," I said, "is the invisible Courtney."

Sean watched Courtney and Rigel for a moment.

"Mom and Dad have to see this," he said. He turned and headed for the house.

A few minutes later, Sean came back with Mr. and Mrs. O'Reilly.

They all watched Rigel and Courtney in amazement.

Finally, after making Rigel do some awesome tricks—including walking sideways doing a kind of dance step—Courtney rode Rigel over to the edge of the paddock and hopped off. She patted Rigel on the nose. Her face was shining. "He's a great horse," she told Mr. and Mrs. O'Reilly.

"You're a great rider," Mrs. O'Reilly said, smiling broadly.

For a second, Courtney looked surprised. She glanced over at me. I gave her a big grin. Slowly, she grinned back.

"Thank you," she said simply, turning to Mrs. O'Reilly. "It's been a while since I've been on a horse."

"Well," Mr. O'Reilly said, "anytime you want to ride Rigel, you're more than welcome."

"I truly think you belong on that animal," Mrs. O'Reilly added. "And he needs you. We need you, in fact. He hasn't looked that good in months."

Courtney's face was glowing. "Thank you," she said quietly. "I'd love to keep riding him. But right now," she said, looking at me, "we've got some work to do."

I nodded.

We certainly did.

We had a horse to cool down . . . and a paper to write.

And now I wouldn't be writing it alone!

Chapter 9

Sunday

Dear Diary,

Well, Diary, last night was the big White Oak auction. And it was a huge success!

But let me back up a bit before I tell you about it. Friday morning, Becky and I went back to the mall to replace the pug dog.

But this time, we had a lot more fun!

At Green's, we found a pug that was actually a little less ugly than Mrs. Kimberley's. It was called Champion Moon.

Then I got Becky to try on clothes with me.

She twirled around at American Alley, modeling a pair of dark jeans and an adorable orange-and-red sweater.

"I'll have to take you shopping when we save up enough money," I told her. "You look great!"

"Thanks." Becky smiled back at me. "And Ashley, thanks for being"—she looked a little surprised—"a good friend. We are friends, aren't we? I hadn't really thought about it. We hardly knew each other before we started working together."

I nodded and grinned. "Yeah. There's nothing

like trouble to cement a friendship! And there's one other thing that can really create a bond that lasts for a lifetime. . . ."

"What's that?" Becky asked.

"Manicures!" I told her.

So we went to Nail Time and spent the rest of the day getting our nails done.

As we were leaving the mall, we ran into my cousin Jeremy, who attends nearby Harrington Academy.

"Hey, Ashley!" he said, looking at Becky. "Who's your friend?"

Becky blushed.

"Becky, this is my cousin Jeremy," I told her. "If you're smart, you'll have nothing to do with him."

Jeremy's eyes lit up. "Becky? Are you the pizza girl?" he asked.

I stared at Jeremy. "What are you talking about?" I said.

"Harrington got a surprise giant pizza delivery last week," he said. "On Tuesday night? And there was a note—something about it being from Becky at White Oak."

Becky and I stared at Jeremy in total shock, our mouths hanging open.

Suddenly, I knew exactly what must have happened. "I'll bet Dana is behind this!" I told Becky. "She probably called Mario's and changed the order. . . ."

"Would Dana do something that mean?" Becky asked.

"You bet she would," I said, nodding. I turned to my cousin. "Thanks, Jeremy. You just helped us solve a little mystery."

"I did?" Jeremy shrugged. "Whatever. It was good pizza."

"Bye," I said to Jeremy, grabbing Becky. "We have a dog to deliver!"

"Huh?" Jeremy looked around for a dog. But we were already out of there.

On Saturday afternoon, Becky came to my room to get ready for the auction. She let me do her hair and pick out her outfit. She looked stunning when I was done, Diary.

The auction was so exciting. There were women in sequined gowns, and men in tuxedos. Waiters offered us fancy little hors d'oeuvres and sparkling juices. Lots of important people came to buy all kinds of items.

It was a big success. The auction made a record amount of money. Becky and I helped out, handing items to Mrs. Pritchard and keeping things organized. Becky did a great job . . . and she looked totally confident of herself for a change.

Mrs. Pritchard was thrilled. "Ashley, Becky," she told us, "we've made more than enough money to build the science lab. And I couldn't have done it without you. Thanks, girls."

As Mrs. Pritchard walked away, I look at Becky. She was glowing! I was pretty pleased myself, too. You've probably guessed by now that we were both going to keep our jobs for the rest of the term!

"Girls?"

I turned around. Standing there was a small gray-haired lady who looked very serious indeed.

"Yes?" I said.

"I wanted to introduce myself," she said. "I'm Mrs. Kimberley."

I must have turned as red as a tomato. "Uh, Mrs. Kimberley, nice to meet you," I stammered.

Becky stood there like she was frozen solid.

"I just wanted you to know," the lady went on seriously, "that I thought my lovely statue might have brought a little more money. Next time, you might want to feature my donation a little more prominently."

I breathed a silent sigh of relief. Mrs. Kimberley

hadn't even noticed that we had replaced her statue! "Of course, Mrs. Kimberley," I said. "I'll make sure to tell Mrs. Pritchard."

When Mrs. Kimberley had moved on, Becky elbowed me in the ribs. "She never even noticed!" she gasped.

Later, in my room, we told Mary-Kate all about the auction.

"Congratulations!" she said. "You guys must have raised a ton of money!"

I nodded. "Mrs. Pritchard says we did pretty well," I said. "But I'm glad it's over. It was a lot of work."

Something in my face must have alerted my sister. "You never shrink from work," she said. "Is there a story here that I don't know about?"

"Yeah," I said. "I'll explain later." I turned to Becky. "Let's just say the auction might have been a real *dog*."

Becky giggled. "You can say that again, Ashley!" she said. "But luckily . . . we're at the *tail* end of it now!"

I cracked up. Mary-Kate looked confused. "Come on," she said, grabbing Becky's arm. "Tell me everything. . . ."

So we did.

Dear Diary,

After the auction, Ashley told me the whole story of what happened to her and Becky and the pug dog.

"I'm really glad things worked out for everybody," I told her this morning. "Becky seems really nice."

"She is," Ashley told me. "So how have you and Courtney been doing?"

I probably looked a little smug. "Guess what grade Courtney and I got on our paper for Ms. Lewis?" I asked my sister.

Ashley looked at me, her eyes twinkling.

"A C?" she said.

"Ashley!" I put my hands on my hips. "Puh-lease!"

Ashley laughed. "Only kidding," she said. "An A?"

"Close," I told her. "We got an A-plus!"

"Mary-Kate!" Ashley squealed, giving me a big hug. "I'm so glad!"

"Me too," I said, hugging her back. "But the best thing about it is how happy Courtney is now that she's riding again. She says she can't imagine how she lived even one day without horses. She loves them so much."

"I knew you could get through to her," Ashley said, giving me another quick hug.

I couldn't help boasting . . . just a little. "Ms. Lewis said our paper was great," I told her. "She heard from the O'Reillys, too, about how we had helped Rigel. She said we had really understood what it was like for a nervous animal who needs patience and support."

"And a little horse sense!" my sister joked.

"Are you calling me a horse?" I said, grinning.

"If the *horseshoe* fits," Ashley hooted.

"I can see I'm going to have to *rein* you in a little," I said, picking up a pillow. "Pillow fight!"

Phoebe, Summer, and Campbell showed up just as we were getting into it, so we had to stop and tell them the whole story . . . and then they told us all about *their* adventures in the animal kingdom.

And *then* we finally had our pillow fight.

But that's a whole other *tail*!

Two of a Kind
"Win a Sterling Silver Charm Bracelet" Sweepstakes
OFFICIAL RULES:

1. NO PURCHASE OR PAYMENT NECESSARY TO ENTER OR WIN.

2. How to Enter. To enter, complete the official entry form or hand print your name, address, age, and phone number along with the words "*Two of a Kind* Win A Sterling Silver Charm Bracelet Sweepstakes" on a 3" x 5" card and mail to: "*Two of a Kind* Win A Sterling Silver Charm Bracelet Sweepstakes" c/o HarperEntertainment, Attn: Children's Marketing Department, 10 East 53rd Street, New York, NY 10022. Entries must be received no later than July 28, 2005. Enter as often as you wish, but each entry must be mailed separately. One entry per envelope. Partially completed, illegible, or mechanically reproduced entries will not be accepted. Sponsor is not responsible for lost, late, mutilated, illegible, stolen, postage due, incomplete, or misdirected entries. All entries become the property of Dualstar Entertainment Group, LLC, and will not be returned.

3. Eligibility. Sweepstakes are open to all legal residents of the United States (excluding Colorado and Rhode Island), who are between the ages of five and fifteen on July 28, 2005 excluding employees and immediate family members of HarperCollins Publishers, Inc., ("HarperCollins"), Parachute Properties and Parachute Press, Inc., and their respective subsidiaries and affiliates, officers, directors, shareholders, employees, agents, attorneys, and other representatives and their immediate families (individually and collectively, "Parachute"), Dualstar Entertainment Group, LLC, and its subsidiaries, affiliates and related companies, officers, directors, shareholders, employees, agents, attorneys, and other representatives and their immediate families (individually and collectively, "Dualstar"), and their respective parent companies, affiliates, subsidiaries, advertising, promotion and fulfillment agencies, and the persons with whom each of the above are domiciled. All applicable federal, state and local laws and regulations apply. Offer void where prohibited or restricted by law.

4. Odds of Winning. Odds of winning depend on the total number of entries received. Approximately 250,000 sweepstakes announcements published. All prizes will be awarded. Winners will be randomly drawn on or about August 15, 2005, by HarperCollins, whose decision is final. Potential winners will be notified by mail and will be required to sign and return an affidavit of eligibility and release of liability within 14 days of notification. Prize won by minors will be awarded to parent or legal guardian who must sign and return all required legal documents. By acceptance of the prize, winners consent to the use of their name, photograph, likeness, and biographical information by HarperCollins, Parachute, Dualstar, and for publicity purposes without further compensation except where prohibited.

5. Grand-Prize. Twenty Grand-Prize Winners will win a sterling silver charm bracelet. Approximate retail value is $100 per prize.

6. Prize Limitations. Prizes are non-transferable and cannot be sold or redeemed for cash. No cash substitute is available. Any federal, state, or local taxes are the responsibility of the winners. Sponsor may substitute prize of equal or greater value, if necessary, due to availability.

7. Additional terms: By participating, entrants agree a) to the official rules and decisions of the judges, which will be final in all respects; and to waive any claim to ambiguity of the official rules and b) to release, discharge, and hold harmless HarperCollins, Parachute, Dualstar, and their respective parent companies, affiliates, subsidiaries, employees and representatives and advertising, promotion and fulfillment agencies from and against any and all liability or damages associated with acceptance, use, or misuse of any prize received or participation in any Sweepstakes-related activity or participation in this Sweepstakes.

8. Dispute Resolution. Any dispute arising from this Sweepstakes will be determined according to the laws of the State of New York, without reference to its conflict of law principles, and the entrants consent to the personal jurisdiction of the State and Federal courts located in New York County and agree that such courts have exclusive jurisdiction over all such disputes.

9. Winner Information. To obtain the name of the winners, please send your request and a self-addressed stamped envelope (residents of Vermont may omit return postage) to "*Two of a Kind* Win A Sterling Silver Charm Bracelet Sweepstakes" Winner, c/o HarperEntertainment, 10 East 53rd Street, New York, NY 10022 after September 15, 2005, but no later than March 15, 2006.

10. Sweepstakes Sponsor: HarperCollins Publishers.

TWO of a kind™ BOOK SERIES

Based on the hit television series

mary-kate olsen ashley olsen

#40 TWO of a kind Diaries

Wish on a Star

www.mary-kateandashley.com

Mary-Kate and Ashley are off to White Oak Academy, an all-girl boarding school in New Hampshire! With new roommates, fun classes, and a boys' school just down the road, there's excitement around every corner!

Don't miss the other books in the TWO of a kind™ book series!

- ❏ It's a Twin Thing
- ❏ How to Flunk Your First Date
- ❏ The Sleepover Secret
- ❏ One Twin Too Many
- ❏ To Snoop or Not to Snoop?
- ❏ My Sister the Supermodel
- ❏ Two's a Crowd
- ❏ Let's Party!
- ❏ Calling All Boys
- ❏ Winner Take All
- ❏ P.S. Wish You Were Here
- ❏ The Cool Club
- ❏ War of the Wardrobes

- ❏ Bye-Bye Boyfriend
- ❏ It's Snow Problem
- ❏ Likes Me, Likes Me Not
- ❏ Shore Thing
- ❏ Two for the Road
- ❏ Surprise, Surprise!
- ❏ Sealed with a Kiss
- ❏ Now You See Him, Now You Don't
- ❏ April Fools' Rules!
- ❏ Island Girls
- ❏ Surf, Sand, and Secrets
- ❏ Closer Than Ever
- ❏ The Perfect Gift

- ❏ The Facts About Flirting
- ❏ The Dream Date Debate
- ❏ Love-Set-Match
- ❏ Making a Splash!
- ❏ Dare to Scare
- ❏ Santa Girls
- ❏ Heart to Heart
- ❏ Prom Princess
- ❏ Camp Rock 'n' Roll
- ❏ Twist and Shout
- ❏ Hocus-pocus
- ❏ Holiday Magic
- ❏ Candles, Cake, Celebrate!

Books for Real Girls